The Perfect Friend

YELENA ROMANOVA
PICTURES BY BORIS KULIKOV

FRANCES FOSTER BOOKS   FARRAR, STRAUS AND GIROUX   NEW YORK

Text copyright © 2005 by Yelena Romanova

Illustrations copyright © 2005 by Boris Kulikov

Distributed in Canada by Douglas & McIntyre Publishing Group

Color separations by Chroma Graphics PTE Ltd.

Printed and bound in the United States of America by Phoenix Color Corporation

Designed by Robbin Gourley

First edition, 2005

1 3 5 7 9 10 8 6 4 2

www.fsgkidsbooks.com

Library of Congress Cataloging-in-Publication Data

Romanova, Yelena, date.

The perfect friend / Yelena Romanova ; pictures by Boris Kulikov.— 1st ed.

p.   cm.

Summary: Archie the dog is unsure about his role in the family when a new baby arrives.

ISBN-13: 978-0-374-35821-1

ISBN-10: 0-374-35821-4

[1. Babies—Fiction.   2. Dogs—Fiction.   3. Friendship—Fiction.]   I. Kulikov, Boris, ill.   II. Title.

PZ7.R66037 Pe 2005

[E]—dc22

2004050635

For Frances
—Y.R.

To Max's grandparents
—B.K.

ONE RAINY DAY, Archie took
a walk alone. He wished he had
a friend to play with, someone
to throw a ball for him to catch. Everybody
had left home that morning promising a
surprise when they returned. What would
it be this time?

Once they brought Archie a goldfish. It was interesting to watch, but it wouldn't play with him.

Then they got him a turtle. But
the turtle was too slow for Archie.

Next came a rabbit—a very hungry rabbit who had no time to be Archie's friend.

Archie dreamed
about something bigger.

Archie's dream was interrupted by a horn.
His family was home.

He ran to open the gate, and in drove the
big yellow car filled with surprises.

Archie wondered which surprise was for him.

He tried them all, but nothing fit.

Then he saw something he hadn't noticed before—a wriggling, snuffling bundle in a cradle.

"Come, Archie," called the parents. "We'd like you to meet Max."

Was this the surprise they'd promised him?

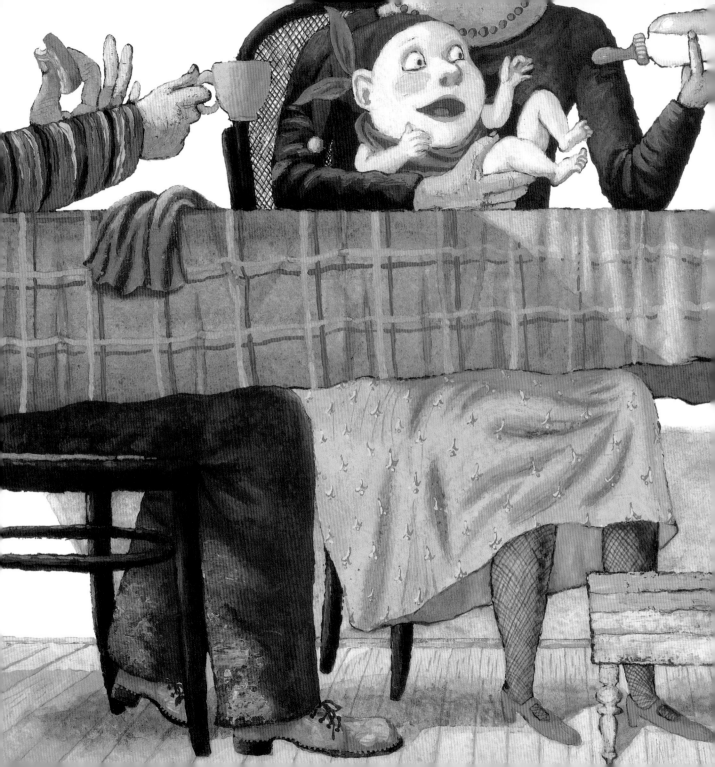

Dinnertime came. Archie took his place at the table, picturing scrambled eggs and ham. He was very hungry. But everybody was so busy feeding Max there was nothing for Archie, not even a scrap.

So Archie did something he
was not supposed to do at all . . .

. . . and then he helped himself to a little snack.

Day after day, Archie watched the people take care of Max, who grew bigger and bigger. They ran to him whenever he cried. They carried him around and sang to him. No one paid any attention to Archie, who felt smaller and smaller.

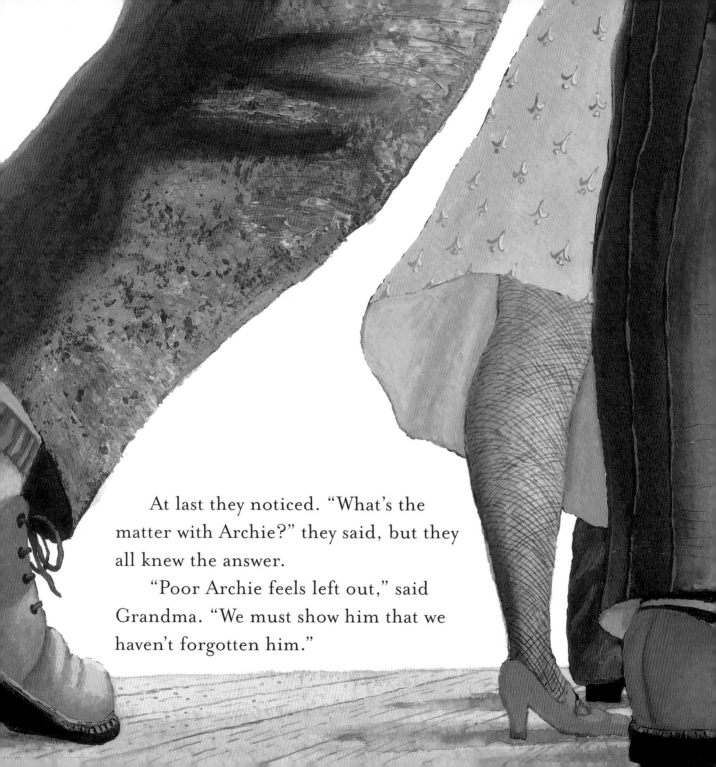

At last they noticed. "What's the matter with Archie?" they said, but they all knew the answer.

"Poor Archie feels left out," said Grandma. "We must show him that we haven't forgotten him."

Grandma played
the piano for him.

Grandpa taught him how to play chess.

Father took him bicycling.

Mother performed a puppet show.

Every day was filled with activities. But something was missing, until one day a ball bounced through the doorway. Archie jumped and turned a happy somersault to catch it. "Yes!" he thought, here was the ball he'd dreamed about—but where was the friend to throw it? And there stood Max . . .

The perfect friend.